T0381422

SHEPHERD'S HAVEN

A Christian Novella

JOAN SELIG

Copyright © 2018 by Joan Selig. 787262

ISBN: Softcover   978-1-9845-6229-6
       EBook   978-1-9845-6228-9

All rights reserved. No part of this book may be reproduced
or transmitted in any form or by any means, electronic or
mechanical, including photocopying, recording, or by any
information storage and retrieval system, without permission
in writing from the copyright owner.

This is a work of fiction. Names, characters, places and
incidents either are the product of the author's imagination
or are used fictitiously, and any resemblance to any actual
persons, living or dead, events, or locales is entirely
coincidental.

Print information available on the last page

Rev. date: 10/24/2018

To order additional copies of this book, contact:
Xlibris
1-888-795-4274
www.Xlibris.com
Orders@Xlibris.com

SHEPHERD'S HAVEN

CHAPTER 1

Streams of sunlight started peeking through Marie's window blind. Marie opened her eyes and smiled. She loved seeing the sun coming through her window. Her rays of hope, she called them. Off flew her covers, and she went to her closet to see what to wear to school. Dressing in her favorite pair of jeans and sweater, she got ready for the day.

She heard her mom and dad talking through her bedroom door. It sounded like the same old conversation, or more accurately, argument. Marie's dad, Ben, was a construction foreman for Adams Construction and worked a lot of long hours. Sometimes he didn't come home until 10:00 or 11:00 pm. These long hours started about three months ago and he had been at odds with Marie's mom, Candace, ever since. He was hardly ever home for dinner and when he was there, he complained that the meatloaf was soggy or the chicken was too tough. Candace tried to keep the apartment clean, but Ben always managed to find a problem. He also smelled of perfume that didn't belong to Candace. Marie was sensing her mom's fear and knew Candace was afraid he was having an affair.

"What time do you think you will be home tonight?" Candace asked Ben.

"I will be home when I get home. Stop bugging me about that. You are such a nag."

"I just want to know if you will have dinner with Marie and I or if I should just keep it warm."

"Do whatever you want. I don't care."

"Would you like tuna casserole or beef stew? I can do either."

"Stop asking me all these questions. You drive me crazy! Forget dinner. I will get some takeout." Ben said angrily and left, slamming the door behind him.

Marie had finished getting dressed and came out of her room. "What's wrong, mommy?"

"Nothing, honey. Your dad was running late and had to leave in a hurry," answered Candace. "What would you like for lunch today? I have bologna or peanut butter."

"Bologna is fine. Do we have any chips left?"

"Sorry baby, we don't, but you can have an apple. Is that okay?"

"That would be great, mom, thanks."

Candace turned around to get Marie her bowl of corn flakes and brushed away a few tears. She was frustrated, not only because Ben was staying away so much, but that finances were so tight. Ben used to make plenty of money and give her enough for household expenses. Nowadays he gave her less and less, or claimed he forgot, and became furious if she reminded him.

She could hardly provide decent meals for her daughter while trying to make the nice dinners Ben used to enjoy but now rarely showed up to eat. Marie tended to be underweight and got sick easily. Ben had health coverage at work, but Candace couldn't afford the co-pays or deductibles with what Ben gave her these days. She had to take Marie to the free clinic around the corner. Candace felt like such a failure as a mom and now also as a wife.

"I'm done with my cereal, mom," said Marie.

"Good job, honey," said Candace. "Go and brush your teeth and brush your pretty red hair."

"Okay, mommy." Marie ran off to the bathroom.

Candace washed the dishes while Marie was getting ready for school. She hated leaving dirty dishes in the sink. Ben had taught her that. He was a real perfectionist. Candace was raised on a farm where everything being spotless was impossible. Everyone was always dragging in dirt, grass, or hay. Candace had loved the farm. It was long days and hard work, but she didn't mind. She had her own animals to take care of and had loved riding on the tractor with her dad. Always, she was there when their cows, pigs, goats, or chickens gave birth to their babies and she had even helped from time to time. It had been quite a change for Candace to go from rural life to living in the city. She had always pictured herself as a farmer's wife, but then she had met Ben.

The town Candace grew up in, Hollow Springs, had a twister come through when she was eighteen that had destroyed most of the downtown. The mayor's office, the fire station, and the local mom and pop stores in the town square were wiped out. There was no construction company in town, so the mayor advertised for the need of one to help rebuild their little town. Adams Construction replied and had the lowest bid.

Candace had learned later that Ben had joined the company out of high school and apprenticed to be a framer and also to work with sheet rock. He had told her that when he had just graduated high school his family had no money for college. Since he was good with his hands Adams had looked like a good fit.

Candace had also just graduated high school, but her only skills were related to the farm. She was a great cook and baker, could milk a cow, gather eggs, grow her own garden, drive a tractor, and harvest crops, but had no office skills and, like Ben's family, hers couldn't afford to send her to school to learn other skills.

Soon after Adams Construction had started building Judy's Jewelry shop, Candace went grocery shopping nearby for bread-making ingredients and saw Ben hoisting up the store frame. She couldn't help but notice how strong he was, and he was quite handsome, too. He was 6' 2", weighed 200 lbs, had wavy blond hair, and was very muscular. She felt embarrassed when he caught her staring at him and ran into the store. While in the store, she ran into the mayor's wife, Marilyn. Candace asked about the construction company and where they came from.

"They are from Homewood." answered Marilyn. "They have a great reputation and built many buildings downtown there."

"That's great," said Candace. "It's wonderful how they are helping us out."

"When they are done, we will have a grand opening ceremony. Everyone in town will be invited and enjoy a potluck dinner afterwards."

"Can't wait."

She paid for her purchases and went outside to see if she could get another glimpse of Ben, but he had gone on break.

Candace went home and started making her bread. Her mom came in from the barn and put a load of laundry into the washer.

"Mom, I saw the construction crew working on Judy's Jewelry shop when I went to the grocery store today," Candace said.

"That's nice, honey. It is so great they are helping us." said Candace's mom Rose.

"That's what I told the mayor's wife in the store. They all look so strong and muscular."

"Oh, anyone in particular you're talking about?"

Candace blushed. "Well, I did notice one about my age who was tall, blond, and very muscular. Don't know his name, though."

"From what I hear, they are suppose to be here for at least six months, so there is plenty of time to find out."

Thanks for the info, mom," giggled Candace." I will finish making the bread now."

At church on Sunday, some of the Adams Construction workers came to the First Baptist Church, where Candace and her family attended, including Ben.

When Candace saw Ben walk in, her heart skipped a beat and started racing. "That's him, mom. He is the one I was talking about."

"Wow. He is really handsome, Candace. I see why you noticed him."

"What do I do? How do I approach him?"

"He's not a movie star. When church lets out just go say hi, thank him for helping our town, and then let God do the rest."

Okay, but I hope my knees stop shaking by then."

After church, Candace found Ben in the crowd and slowly went his direction. As she approached him, he turned around, saw her, and smiled.

"You're the girl I saw a few days ago when I was working. You went into the grocery store," Ben said.

"Yeah I am. I am embarrassed. I didn't mean to stare, but you seem so strong and I was impressed," Candace said, blushing.

"Thanks. My dad had weights in the garage and I have lifted weights since middle school. Construction work seemed like a good career move for me."

"I am glad to see you here in church," Candace said.

"Well, I need to flex my spiritual muscles, too."

Candace laughed. "I never thought of it that way. I guess we all need to. Well, my parents are walking out of the church. By the way, what is your name?" asked Candace.

"Ben. Ben Morgan and what's yours?" Ben asked.

"Candace. Candace Willows. Glad to meet you, Ben Morgan."

"Likewise," Ben said. "Hope to see you next Sunday."

"You can count on it, Ben."

"Well, how did it go?" Rose asked Candace when she joined them.

"How did what go?" asked Candace's dad Bert.

"Oh, our daughter has a crush one of the construction workers, Bert. He was at church and she went over to talk to him," Rose explained.

"Mom, you are embarrassing me." Candace protested.

Well, isn't it the truth?" Rose asked.

"I guess it is, but it is still embarrassing," Candace replied.

"Would someone please tell me what is going on?" asked Bert.

"Dad, I saw Ben working at Judy's Jewelry shop the other day and though he was really cute. He happened to come into church this morning and mom encouraged me to go and talk to him. He is really nice and plans on coming to church next week, too. Could we maybe invite him over for lunch after church?" asked Candace.

"Ben?" asked Rose.

"Yes, mom. His name is Ben Morgan. So, can he come to lunch, please?" Candace begged.

"You encouraged her to go over to him? What were you thinking? We know nothing about him," said Bert.

"Well, what better way to get to know him than by talking to him and inviting him to lunch next Sunday?" exclaimed Rose.

"Thank you, thank you, thank you, mom." Candace squealed with delight. "Is it okay, dad?" asked Candace.

"Okay, okay, but this isn't fair. It is two against one," said Bert.

"Thanks, dad." Candace as she hugged her dad around his neck.

Next Sunday couldn't come fast enough, but it finally arrived. Candace went through her whole closet at least twice to find the right outfit. She finally settled on her white lace skirt and ruffled royal blue top. Rose let her wear her pearls and white pumps.

"Mom, is the chicken ready to be fried when we get back? Is the salad ready? How did the apple pie come out? Candace asked anxiously.

"Calm down, honey. Everything will be great. Just relax and enjoy the day," said Rose calmly.

"I'll try. Thanks, mom. I love you."

Love you, too, baby. Let's get to church."

"Ben, these are my mom and dad, Rose and Bert. After church, we would like for you to join us at our house for lunch," Candace said.

"Nice to meet you both and I would love to accept your invitation. Thank you very much," Ben said.

"That's great, Ben. Hope you like fried chicken and apple pie," Rose said.

"Oh, yes ma'am. Sounds great." Ben grinned.

Ben sat with Candace and her parents during the service and Rose noticed he had a pretty good singing voice. Candace and Ben kept sneaking glances at each other. They were more focused on each other than the pastor and his message, which was titled "God works in mysterious ways."

After church was over, Ben got into his truck and followed Candace and her parents to their farm.

"You have a very nice farm, Mr. and Mrs. Willows," said Ben.

"Thanks, Ben" said Bert. "We are very proud of it."

"Who is ready for lunch?" asked Rose.

"I sure am, how about you, Ben?" asked Bert.

"Absolutely. Smells great."

Everyone sat down at the table and Candace said grace. At the beginning, there was more eating than talking, but finally Bert asked, "so Ben, tell us about your family."

"Well, I grew up in the city with my sister and brother. My dad was a factory worker and mom was a housewife. Dad worked really hard, but didn't make much money, so it was a struggle. Most of our clothes came from thrift shops and we had to go to food banks." said Ben.

"That sounds tough," replied Bert.

"It was, but we managed. My brother and sister were older and they managed to go to a community college, but there was no money for me to go. I wasn't really book smart and was better with my hands, so that's why I joined Adams Construction out of high school and got into their apprentice program. It's been good. I'm happy there."

"Well, it looks like you're doing all right," said Rose.

"I am, but I hope someday to be able to get married and have a family. I make a pretty decent wage and I'm a pretty handy man around the house."

Candace blushed with this announcement, but was secretly leaping for joy inside.

When lunch was over, Rose and Candace started clearing the table and washing the dishes. Bert and Ben went into the family room to watch a ball game.

"So, mom, what do you think of Ben?" asked Candace.

"He seems real nice and a responsible young man," replied Rose.

"I really like him, mom. I feel alive around him and think about him all the time since I met him. I can even see marrying him someday."

"That's great, Candace, but let's slow down. I want you to be happy, but don't rush into a serious relationship too fast."

"I know, mom, but it's hard," admitted Candace.

"Well, let's just see where this goes."

Ben and Candace were joined at the hip for the next six months. Whenever Ben was off work, they were together. They went out to eat, to the movies, took long walks, went to every local event, and Ben was over at Candace's house for every Sunday lunch. Time was running out, though, for Ben to be there in Hollow Springs. Ben's boss had stated they were ahead of schedule on finishing all the projects and should be done in another two weeks. This was not good news for Ben and Candace.

"I can't believe you will be gone in two weeks. What are we going to do?" asked Candace.

"Well, I know it is pretty fast, but what if we get married?" replied Ben.

"Really?" Candace squealed with delight. "That would make me so happy, but I'm not sure how my parents will feel about this."

"I think we should ask them at Sunday lunch. What do you think?"

"That would be the perfect time, Ben. I am nervous, but so happy at the same time." Candace gave Ben a long kiss and said, "Until then, my love.

When Sunday came, Candace paced nervously around the house before church.

"Is everything all right, Candace?" You seem upset about something. Is there a problem with Ben?

"No, mom. We are great. Everything is okay. Let's get to church. Don't want to be late," replied Candace. She caught her mother's *I know something's up* look.

"Okay, let's go."

Church was uneventful, and Candace was so nervous she couldn't think of anything to say in the car on the way home.

"Are you sure everything is all right, Candace? You were so quiet in church and in the car," said Rose.

"I'm fine, mom. Let's just get lunch started."

"Okay, but I'll find out what's up with you."

"Yes you will," said Candace under her breath.

Lunch was quiet as well and both Ben and Candace were squirming in their seats.

"Okay, you, two. What is going on?" demanded Rose.

Ben cleared his throat and said, "Well, Candace and I have an announcement. Since my time here is coming to an end, we have decided to get married and would like your approval. We are so happy together and can't think of being apart. We know we have only known each other six months, but we know we want to be together. We hope you will agree to this. We really want your blessing."

Stunned, Rose said, "Wow, no wonder both of you have been acting strangely."

Bert said, "Candace, you have grown up on a farm. Do you think you can handle city life?"

"Yes, it will be a big change for me, but I can do it with Ben's help," replied Candace. "I know this is fast, but I really want this. I love Ben so much and he loves me. I know he will be good to me."

Or so Candace thought.

CHAPTER 2

"Where is everybody?" Linda Metzler called out. "Breakfast is ready and we need to get going."

First Lance, Linda's husband, appeared in the kitchen, followed by their children, Maggie and Matthew.

"Take it easy, mom. The bus doesn't come for half an hour," said Matthew.

"Well, I have a meeting in twenty minutes and can't be late," Linda replied.

"Are you going to be at my game tonight, mom? It starts at 6:30. The coach said I will get some play time tonight," said Matthew.

"Oh, is that tonight? I can't. I have a client dinner tonight at 6:00. I will come to the next one, Matt."

"That's what you said the last time," Matthew complained.

"I can make it, buddy," said his father.

"Can I come, too?" asked Maggie.

"Of course you can," Lance said.

"See? Everything is okay," said Linda.

"Yeah, sure mom," Matthew grumbled.

"Why do you do that to Matt?" asked Lance.

"Do what?" inquired Linda.

"Put him second to your job. You've only made it to one game and it's important to him to have his family there supporting him." replied Lance.

"You guys will be there, and my job keeps a decent roof over our heads."

"Are you implying my income isn't enough?".

"You are an architect. There are so many big condo projects that you could bid for, but you choose the low-income refabs. You could do so much better." replied Linda.

"It is not always about money. I feel what I do is more important than building more condos for the rich."

"Your platform for the poor won't get our kids into college. I am doing that and it is getting old. I need your help."

"The kids may not get into Harvard or Yale, but they will get a college education and that's what is important."

"What's wrong with Harvard or Yale?"

"Nothing, but there a lot of good colleges closer that will offer a good education. We don't have to kill ourselves to get them into the highest tuition college."

"Oh, of course, Bradford Community College looks much better on a resume than Harvard and Yale. Employers appreciate a cheap education." Linda's sarcasm wasn't at all subtle.

"Just go to your meeting. Have a good day."

"Fine, whatever. You, too. Go make nice with the homeless," retorted Linda, and slammed out the door.

"I will."

The school bus horn sounded. Matthew and Maggie grabbed their lunches and ran out the door.

"Have a good day," yelled Lance as he headed for his car.

In her office building, Linda ran into Sam's Café for some coffee and caught the elevator to the 11th floor to get to her office in the Lawler & Stockton Brokerage Firm. Her secretary Marge had already put a stack of messages on her desk.

"Mr. Richards really needs to talk to you ASAP. He has called three times already this morning," said Marge.

"I will get to him as soon as I can. I have other calls to make first," said Linda.

"Okay, but if he calls again, I am putting him right through. He is definitely upset about something."

"He should never invest in the stock market. He doesn't have the stomach for it. He is worried that his Noviton stock has gone down 20%. It will rebound, but he wants to sell. Wimp."

"I probably would want to sell, too."

"Well, it is a good thing you don't invest then." retorted Linda.

"I need a new job." Marge said under her breath.

Lance arrived at his office and sorted through his messages. One caught his eye from Daniel Davis, president of the low income housing coalition. He wanted to buy several rundown homes to refab with funds he received from a grant and planned to rent them to low income families. This was the kind of project Lance loved, much to the disgust of Linda. She wanted him to design huge condo complexes and malls to make big money. Lance was not opposed to money, but knew how it felt to struggle financially. His dad was a bus driver and his mom worked in a laundromat. They had always lived paycheck to paycheck, something Linda had never had to do. Her father was a prestigious doctor and her mother owned her own business and was a successful businesswoman like Linda. Lance sometimes wondered why Linda ever married him. He had just graduated with a degree in architecture and he always assumed he would take on big projects worth millions of dollars. Lance had started doing that when he opened his own firm, but soon realized how empty he felt when only dealing with the rich. He wanted to make a difference for low income people. That's when problems started with Linda. This issue seemed to be a daily argument now.

The bell rang ending third period and Matthew Metzler ran to his locker because he forgot his Algebra book for fourth period. On the way to class, his basketball coach Mr. Reynolds caught up to him.

"Hey, Matthew. Just wanted to remind you will definitely get some playtime tonight. Jimmy Sanders sprained his ankle and I will need you as point guard."

"Sorry about Jimmy, but thanks for the playtime. I will do my best," said Matthew.

"Will your family be here tonight?' asked Mr. Reynolds.

"Well, my dad and sister will be, but my mom has to work."

"Seems like your mom is always working."

"She is. Sometimes I think she loves money more than us."

"Sorry to hear that. That is a very common problem, though."

"I wish I could get her to understand I don't need a new iPad. I just want to send time as a family."

"I hope you will get through to her someday."

"Thanks. Got to get to class. Big Algebra test today."

"Okay. Good luck on the test and with your mom."

Maggie Metzler ran into the music room to her orchestra practice. She started putting together her flute and put her music on the music stand. She didn't think she had practiced the piece enough at home so she worked on it until her music teacher Mrs. Burns came in.

"Okay, everyone," said Mrs. Burns. "Put your instruments down for the moment. I have an announcement to make. I have decided who will do the solos for the piece. Thomas Allen will do the trumpet solo, Brian Kelly will do the trombone solo, Alisha Smith will do the clarinet solo, and Brittney Jones will do the flute solo. Now, let's get started."

After practice, Maggie went to lunch. She had her usual PB&J, potato chips, and an apple. Maggie was pretty shy and didn't have many friends. She sat in the back of the lunchroom and as she ate, she tried not to cry. She had really wanted to do the flute solo. She hadn't been practicing enough, though, and she knew it. Her mom Linda never came to the recitals, and sometimes she thought, *What's the point?* Her dad Lance and brother Matthew tried to come when they could, but the family was never complete. That bothered Maggie. She hoped someday her whole family would attend.

"Mrs. Metzler, Mr. Richards is on the phone again. Could you please talk to him?" asked Marge.
"Okay, okay. Put him on." said Linda.

"Mrs. Metzler, I have left you several messages. I want to sell my shares of Noviton. It keeps going down and I don't want to lose anymore money. Please sell them," asked Mr. Richards.

"Now, Mr. Richards, I have told you before that stocks will go up and down, but you shouldn't panic. This stock is sound and will rebound, but you have to be patient."

"I don't want to be patient. I want to sell."

"Okay, I will, but maybe you should consider doing other investments. The stock market may not be for you."

"I am staying in the stock market, but I've gotten another broker. You are too aggressive for me."

"That's how you make money, Mr. Richards."

"It's also how you can lose it, Mrs. Metzler."

Lance had lunch with Daniel Davis to get the details on his project.

"I'm glad you requested my firm to do your project. This sounds great," said Lance.

"I am glad you'll do it. Most firms won't touch it because of the money, or lack of it." replied Mr. Davis.

"I know. My wife wishes I would only go after huge money contracts, but the low income need good and safe housing, too, and I am happy to help."

"The purchase of these homes should be finalized in two more weeks, and then I would like to start." said Mr. Davis.

"I will get started on the drawings right away."

"That is great. I look forward to our next meeting."

Matthew went into the locker room to get dressed for the game. He was a little nervous since he would get some play time, but also excited. He knew his dad and sister would be there, but was secretly hoping to see his mom, too. He really wanted her to see how he had improved.

"All right, everyone, come on over and listen up. Jimmy Sanders has sprained his ankle and Matthew Metzler will be covering for him. I know we are the underdog, but I have great confidence in all of you. We are playing on our home court and I believe we will have a great game. Go Tigers!" said Coach Reynolds. Everyone in the locker room exploded in applause.

The players ran out onto the court and all the fans in the stands started cheering. Matthew looked up into the stands and saw his dad and sister. They waved to him and he waved back, but was disappointed at not seeing his mother. He wasn't going to allow that to interfere with his game, though. The team was counting on him.

In the first quarter, Matthew didn't play. His team was staying pretty well toe to toe with the Spartans, but Coach Reynolds wanted to shake things up. At the beginning of the second quarter, Matthew got the nod. He was on fire. The Spartans only got ten points all quarter.

Lance and Maggie were going hoarse with all the yelling and cheers. At halftime, the Tigers were ahead by six points. Jubilation filled the locker room.

"I am very proud of all you. You are doing a great job on both offense and defense, but there is room for improvement. We need to improve our percentage at the foul line and you defenders need to be more aggressive and try to create more turnovers. Let's go out there and finish the job. Go Tigers!"

"Yeah!" shouted the team members in unison.

The second half started off a little slow, but picked up in the fourth quarter. Coach Reynolds had Matthew sit out in the third quarter, but put him back in the fourth. He picked up where he left off. He was having his best game ever. The Tigers won 56 to 52. The whole gymnasium went wild.

"You did so great tonight!" said Lance and Maggie.

"Thanks," Matthew said. "I just wish mom was here. She works too much."

I know, son. I will talk to her."

"It's okay, dad." Matthew said. Lance knew it wasn't okay and realized how much it bothered him when Linda put her work before her family. Something was going to have to change.

CHAPTER 3

It was almost 4:00 pm and Candace knew Marie would be home from school soon. Candace had spent the day cleaning the apartment and was making a new recipe for dinner to try and please Ben. The door flung open and Marie came running in.

"Is everything okay, Marie?" asked Candace.

"That darn Billy Daniels was giving me a hard time after school because I wouldn't let him cheat off my math test. He started chasing me and I ran all the way home," explained Marie.

"Well, I want to talk to your teacher about him."

"It's okay, mom. I already told my teacher about it and she is going to talk to his mother."

"I hope that helps, or I will put in my two cents worth." Candace stated.

"Do you want to help me with dinner? I am trying something different tonight."

"Yeah. I hope daddy likes it. He hasn't been home much for dinner lately."

"I know, honey. He has been working late a lot lately." Candace tried to disguise her pain.

Marie went into her room to put her backpack away. "Wow, mom. You did a great job cleaning today. I am sure daddy will be pleased."

"I hope so."

"Mommy, why is daddy so angry all the time?"

"I wish I knew. If it's something I could change, I would, but I don't know what's bothering him. He didn't used to be this way. When we first got married, he was so kind and loving."

"When did things change?" asked Marie.

"Well … after you were born, I think, but it isn't your fault. We got married very young and I guess he wasn't really ready to be a husband and a father. He didn't get to sow his wild oats so to speak. I think that is what he is doing now. I hope he gets this out of his system so we can go back to being a family again."

"Me, too, mommy." said Marie.

Candace and Marie had prepared a delicious dinner and even put out the candles and tablecloth. Candace put on her best dress and put her hair up. Ben was supposed to be home by 6:00, but it was already 7:30 and no sign of him, so Candace cleaned up the dishes and sent Marie off to do her homework.

Marie came back in the kitchen a few minutes later. "Mommy, I can hear you crying. It's because of Daddy, isn't it? I'm going to talk to him when he gets home and see if he's mad at me or something. I know it can't be you. You try so hard to do what he wants."

Candace hated to see her daughter so upset. She knew whatever was wrong wasn't Marie's fault.

Marie worked on her book report of *Treasure Island* and did some math problems, but fell asleep before Ben got home. He finally arrived after midnight and was in no mood for talking.

"Where have you been? Marie and I were so worried," asked Candace.

"Well, I am home know, so stop worrying," Ben answered.

"Who is she? And don't insult me by saying there isn't someone because I know there is." Candace exploded.

"Yeah, there is someone, but it's none of your business who."

"So when were you going to tell me?" Candace asked, trying to hold back the tears.

"I wasn't going to." retorted Ben.

"So now what?"

"I am leaving tomorrow. I am tired of all your nagging and I stopped loving you a long time ago."

"What about Marie and I? What are we suppose to do? cried Candace.

"Get a job, I guess. I can't support you two and pay my bills, too."

"I don't have job skills. I was raised on a farm and then became your wife. What can I do?"

"Well, do what you want. Don't come after me for money or I will take Marie and you won't ever see her again."

"I can't believe you're doing this. What did I ever do to you to deserve this?"

"I should have never married you so young. You could never keep a house clean, cook right, or make love to satisfy me. I found someone who can do all these things."

"What about Marie? Don't you care about her at all?"

"You were the one who wanted kids, not me."

"You bastard!" yelled Marie.

Ben threw some clothes in a suitcase and left, slamming the door behind him. The noise woke Marie up and she came into Candace's room and found her crying.

"What's wrong, mommy?" asked Marie.

"Oh, Marie. Your daddy has left us. I don't know what we are going to do. I guess tomorrow I have to look for a job. All I have is $30.00 in my purse. You daddy has the checkbook and debit card."

"It will be okay, mommy. We are together. We'll figure it out." Marie said giving Candace a big hug.

"Thanks, honey. Go back to bed and get some sleep. You still have to go to school tomorrow."

"Okay, mommy. You get some sleep, too."

"I will." Candace said, but all she could do was cry all night.

Lance got the long-awaited call from Daniel Davis. The properties were purchased and Lance was to start right away on the drawings to rehab these homes. They were all two bedroom cottages on the south side of town. They used to belong to Nash Manufacturing when they had their plant open back in the 90's. They made VCRs and cassette players, but when DVDs and CDs came on the scene, their business really dried up. These homes were where the employees stayed to save travel time. When the plant closed, the homes were abandoned and were not taken care of. Since taxes weren't being paid, the city took them over for a project they had in mind, but never moved forward with it, so they sat for years until Mr. Davis approached the city about taking them over to provide housing for low income families. The city was more than happy to get them off their hands, so the sale went through without a hitch. Lance had his work cut out for him. They were in shambles and will need much work, but Lance has always loved a challenge. He pictured children playing out in the yards and families having barbeques and that really motivated him, unlike Linda, who was always looking the next big stock deal. He wondered how they ever got together sometimes. He really wanted her to enjoy life and her family and not be so motivated by money.

Maggie had just got home when Linda called home to say she would be late, but not to wait for her for dinner. Maggie considered herself a pretty good cook, so she started to make spaghetti for the family.

"Why are you cooking?' asked Matthew when he entered the kitchen.

"Mom called and said she would be late, so I am starting dinner."

"I can't even remember the last time we all ate dinner together."

"I know what you mean. I almost feel like we live in a one-parent household."

"Sometimes I wish we were. At least then we wouldn't be let down so much." Matthew's sadness showed on his face.

"Don't say that," Maggie snapped.

"I'm sorry, but that's how I feel sometimes."

Well, something will happen to turn mom around. You wait and see." Maggie sounded desperate, even to herself.

"I hope you're right, but I'm not going to hold my breath."

"Dad should be home around six and dinner should be ready by then."

"Sounds good to me." Matthew opened up his history book.

Marie got home from school and found Candace looking at the want ads in the paper.

"How did job hunting go today, mom?" asked Marie.

"Not very good. I don't have any office skills, and to be a waitress, they want you to have prior experience. Tomorrow I will check a few factories that are hiring. Maybe I will have better luck there. How was your day, honey?"

"Okay. I got a 90 on my spelling test."

"That's wonderful! I don't want you to be like me and have no work skills. You pay attention in school and you can get a good job someday."

"I will mommy. What was daddy like before I was born? Was he always so grumpy?"

"No, baby. He used to be very loving and sweet to me. He would bring me flowers and we would go out to eat and go to the movies, but when I told him I was pregnant with you, things changed. I don't want you to think this is your fault because it isn't, but we got married very young and your daddy wasn't ready for a family yet. I think he wanted to be able to do what he wanted longer and not have a baby to raise."

"I am glad I have you, mommy. I love you so much." Marie said with tears in her eyes.

"I love you, too, baby. I will take care of you no matter what." promised Candace. Now, let's have some dinner. I am famished."

"I am, too, mommy." Marie said rubbing her stomach.

Candace fell asleep on the couch after looking at the job ads over and over again. She really wished she had gone to college or at least gone to secretarial school. There were so many office positions available, but she had no qualifications. She started dreaming of when she and Ben first got married.
"Are you sure about this, Candace?" Rose asked.

"Oh yes, mom. I love Ben so much. I want to marry him."

"You have always lived on a farm. How are you going to handle living in the city?"

"I know it will be a big adjustment, but Ben will help me."

"I hope so. You know I just want the best for you."

"I know, mom. Ben is the best for me." Candace giggled.

"Okay, then. Let's get you ready for your wedding.

Bert had made a gazebo for the backyard for the wedding. Candace had decorated it with netting and strings of lights and flowers and put satin bows on the chairs. Fortunately it was a beautiful day. Candace wore a simple white satin gown with the same flowers as in the gazebo and Ben wore his best black suit. Candace met Ben's parents at the wedding and they fell in love with her. Candace's pastor performed the ceremony. It was a perfect day.

"I am so happy for you both," said Bert and Rose together.

"Thanks, mom and dad. I am so happy right now, but I will miss you both, too. I love you so much and want to thank you for being the best parents ever. I want to thank you, too, Mr. and Mrs. Morgan, for raising Ben right. I will try to be the best wife for him." said Candace, glowing.

"We know you will, dear," said Mr. and Mrs. Morgan.

"Well, time to go, Candace. Thanks, Mr. and Mrs. Willows, for everything. I will take good care of her," said Ben.

"Thanks, Ben. If you need anything, please don't hesitate to call." Bert said.

"Will do," Ben replied.

The new Mr and Mrs. Morgan drove down the driveway and disappeared around the corner.

"Did we just allow our daughter to ruin her life?" inquired Bert.

"I hope not. Time will tell. Let's clean up, Bert," said Rose.

CHAPTER 4

Candace woke on the couch, not realizing at first where she was.

"Morning, mommy. Didn't you go to bed last night?" asked Marie.

"I guess I fell asleep on the couch. I dreamed about my wedding to your daddy. It was such a perfect day. Never thought it would turn into this."

"Tell me about that day, mommy." Marie asked.

"I will do better. I have our wedding album. Let me show you."

"Oh, mommy. You were so pretty. Is that daddy?" Marie pointed to a picture.

"Yes it is. He was so handsome. I loved him very much."

"Your grandfather made that gazebo. He was very talented that way. I was very blessed to have such great parents. I am so sad they are both gone now. They would have loved to see you grow up."

Candace wiped away a tear. "At least they didn't see what has happened to Ben and I. They warned me we were getting married too young, but I wouldn't listen. I was bound and determined to prove them wrong, but I was the one who was wrong. The best thing to happen was you, Marie. I never regretted having you and I am so proud you are my daughter." Candace squeezed Marie's hand.

"Now, it's time for you to get ready for school and for me to apply for a job at Jackson's Manufacturing. I hope they will hire me."

"They will mommy. You have to have faith." announced Marie.

"Oh, I haven't had faith in a long time, but I guess now would be a good time to get it back," replied Candace.

"Yes it would, mommy," Marie said

Candace walked two miles to Jackson's Manufacturing because she didn't have money for a cab or bus. She had been giving all the cash she had to Marie for lunches. Candace went into the restroom to freshen up. Afterwards, she went up to the third floor and checked in with the receptionist before her interview with Mr. Harvey in Human Resources.

"Mr. Harvey is with another applicant, but will be with you shortly," said the receptionist.

"Thank you." Candace tried to read some magazines but couldn't concentrate. She needed this job so badly.

"Mrs. Morgan? I am Mr. Harvey. Please come in." said Mr. Harvey. "How are you today?" asked Mr. Harvey.

"I'm fine, thank you," replied Candace.

"I see you have no prior work experience. What have you been doing?"

"I have been a housewife and mother. My husband just left us and I need a job in the worst way. I know I have no work experience, but I learn quickly. I will do whatever it takes. Please give me a chance." pleaded Candace.

"Do you have transportation?"

"I would have to walk right now, but when I start getting paychecks, I can take the bus."

"I do have one entry level position at the end of the assembly line looking for defects on assorted parts we manufacture for cars. We will train you what to look for. It is minimum wage, but is full-time and benefits are available. Are you interested?" asked Mr. Harvey.

"Oh, yes! Thank you so much." Candace didn't try to keep the excitement out of her voice. "When can I start?"

"How about tomorrow? Be here at 8:00 am sharp. Bring a lunch. Lunch breaks are 30 minutes, so no time to go out. Day ends usually at 5:00 pm, but sometimes you may be required to stay longer. Okay?" said Mr. Harvey.

"Okay. Thank you again. I will be here tomorrow." Candace left with a spring in her step.

"Thank you, God." prayed Candace.

You are welcome, but stay close to Me. You will still need my help." said a still, small voice.

CHAPTER 5

Six months passed after Candace got her job at Jackson's Manufacturing. Even though she was very grateful to have a job, working at minimum wage with a child was very difficult. Because she needed to buy food and have transportation money to get back and forth to work, she was two months behind on rent. She also had to keep up with the utilities and had to get new clothes to wear at work. There wasn't enough left in her paycheck to cover everything and her landlord threatened eviction if she wasn't caught up by the end of the month. She was very worried about being put out onto the street. Candace talked to her boss about a raise or to see if she could get more hours.

"I sympathize with your situation," said Mr. Albert Harris, Candace's supervisor, "but we are actually looking to cut back on staff due to lower sales of our parts. There has been a reduction in car sales for the past three months. My boss has asked me to let five employees go and, unfortunately, you will have to be one of them since you have only been here six months. I am so sorry, Candace. You are a good worker and I hate to lose you. You can finish out the day and you will get your last paycheck before you leave. Again, I am sorry."

Candace was devastated. Now what should she do? She had no one to help and had nowhere to go. How would she tell Marie they would have to go to a shelter or live on the streets? Candace was at a loss.

Lance Metzler had presented Daniel Davis his drawings for the refab project three months ago and, after some adjustments, construction had started last month. There were twenty cottages to upgrade. Daniel was hoping the project will be completed in nine months' time. He has been contacting several appliance stores in the city to see if they would be willing to donate some stoves, talked to plumbing companies for sinks, tubs, and toilets, and paint from paint stores. Some said yes and some no, but he was hopeful everything would be ready by next spring. He hoped he could round up some landscapers to lay sod and plant some flowers. Lance and Daniel were very excited and planned on advertising these cottages by next April.

CHAPTER 6

It was an especially cold night last night for Candace and her daughter Marie. The cardboard box they call home suffered some major tears due to the stronger than usual wind gusts. Marie had been whimpering periodically through the night about her ears hurting. When daybreak came, she was crying constantly and Candace didn't know what to do.

"Mommy, make then stop hurting, please," begged Marie.

"I want to. I want to honey, but I don't know how." cried Candace.

Falling on her knees, Candace folded her hands and started praying.

"God, you know when my husband left, when I lost my job, and even when Marie and I were evicted from our apartment, I didn't ask for anything from you, but right now I am at my wits end. I can't help my little girl and I am asking you to intervene on her behalf. I don't want anything for myself, but please help Marie."

No sooner had Candace finished praying that Marie screamed in pain and ran down the alley they called home onto First Street. As she stepped off the curb, Linda Metzler was turning left onto First Street on her way to work. Her office building was three blocks from the alley where Candace and Marie lived. Linda, as usual, was on her cell phone selling and trading, when she suddenly saw Marie dart in front of her car. Linda slammed on her brakes, but couldn't avoid hitting Marie. Linda immediately stopped and got out to see if she was all right. Marie was crying, but didn't appear seriously hurt. Linda didn't want to take any chances and called 911 on her cell phone.

"911, what is your emergency?"

"I hit a little girl by accident with my car at the corner of First Street and Fifth Avenue," said Linda.

"Is she breathing? Is she seriously hurt?"

"She is breathing and doesn't appear to be hurt very badly, but I still want her checked out at the hospital," Linda said.

"Okay. There is an ambulance on the way. If you have a blanket, cover her to keep her warm and try to keep her from moving."

"I will, thanks."

Linda covered Marie with a blanket and tried to calm her down. Candace came around the corner, trying to find Marie, and saw all the commotion, so she went over to see what was going on. She gasped when she saw Marie lying on the sidewalk.

"Marie! Marie, are you all right?" screamed Candace.

"Are you her mother?" Linda asked.

"Yes," Candace answered.

"I am so sorry. She came out of nowhere and I couldn't stop in time. I called 911, so an ambulance should be here any minute," Linda explained.

"Mommy, I hurt and I'm scared," Marie said, trying to stop crying.

"I know, honey. Mommy's here. I won't leave you." Candace tried to comfort her daughter.

"If you give me your name, address, and phone number, my insurance agent will contact you and take care of all the expenses." Linda said.

Candace was quiet for a moment, but finally admitted, "Miss, my daughter and I are homeless. We live in a cardboard box in the alley between Broadway and Main Street."

Linda stared in disbelief. She had worked three blocks away for the past ten years in a posh office building with spiral staircases, fountains, and many other luxury amenities and had no idea there were people living on the street nearby.

"How long have you been homeless?" Linda inquired.

"For the past six months. My husband left Marie and me a year ago. The factory I worked at laid me off and then closed. I tried to find other work, but I am not very skilled. My landlord evicted us and we have been on the streets ever since. It's hard to get a job when you have no address or phone number."

"Does Marie go to school?" asked Linda.

"Not any more. She helps me ask for money so we can eat."

The ambulance pulled up and the paramedics examined Marie.

"Fortunately, she doesn't appear to have any broken bones or internal injuries – just some bumps and bruises and scrapes," the paramedic said.

Linda asked the paramedics to take her to Memorial hospital to be checked out anyway and signed forms that she would take care of the bill. Candace went with them. The police arrived as the ambulance pulled away and took Linda's statement, but issued no tickets. Linda got back in her car and went to her office. She was still in shock after all that had just happened. She finally checked her emails and sent some replies, and then called the hospital to check on Marie.

The ER doctor reported that she wasn't seriously injured, but also said she had a severe ear infection, which needed treatment with antibiotics and pain medicine. Since Candace had no means to pay for the prescriptions, Linda was asked to cover this expense. She eagerly agreed and instructed that when Marie was released, a cab should be called to take them to the Victoria Motel.

Linda had a lunch meeting with her bosses and a potential customer at Carlos' restaurant downtown. As she entered the front door, the smells of authentic Mexican cuisine filled the air. Everyone seemed to be enjoying their fajitas, enchiladas, and burritos. As Linda was seated, she reached for the chips and homemade salsa on the table and as she ate, she suddenly wondered if Candace and Marie had ever enjoyed Mexican food. She still couldn't fathom how they had survived all this time on the street. As she glanced around the room, she noticed for the first time a picture of Jesus with a small lamb and the Twenty-third Psalm inscribed underneath. *Carlos must be a Christian*, Linda thought. Linda hadn't read the Bible much, but was familiar with the Twenty-third Psalm. She quoted the first verse to herself. "The Lord is my shepherd. I shall not want." *I shall not want*. Linda surely wasn't in want, but what about Candace or Marie? How would Jesus meet their needs? As if someone had whispered something in her ear, she heard, *"Open Shepherd's Haven."*

CHAPTER 7

Linda got back to her office and kept wondering: *What does Shepherd's Haven mean and where did that thought come from?* Getting out the phone book, she looked up homeless shelters and was shocked to find only one listed. She called them and was surprised to learn they only had thirty beds for men and forty beds for women and children. Because of the large homeless population, they could only house each person for two weeks, after which people had to move on.

Linda couldn't believe this. Suddenly, she had a wild thought. She called her real estate agent to see what buildings might be vacant and be zoned for another homeless shelter. Her agent, Marty Glenn, went right to work on this and faxed Linda a list of ten possibilities. Linda looked them over and over again, and as if someone was whispering to her, when she came across a building on Second Avenue, she heard, *"Buy this one."* She didn't know what was happening, but she faxed back a bid to Marty for this property. Linda just sat stunned in her chair. *This just isn't like me!* She tried to call Lance, but he was on site and not available. Marty called Linda back about an hour later and asked her if she could meet him at 4:00 pm.

"Why?" asked Linda.

"Well, I have never in all my twenty years of being a real estate agent seen a deal go through like this. It really is a miracle. Your bid has been approved and they would like you to sign the papers at 4:00 pm. Is this possible?" asked Marty.

"Oh my gosh! I never expected this. I have been trying to get hold of Lance to let him know about this. I will call you back as soon as I reach him," replied Linda.

"Okay, I will tell them. Get back to me as soon as you can," said Marty.

"I will."

Even though she hadn't told Lance yet, an unexplainable warmth and peace came over Linda. She felt for the first time in her life that what she was doing counted for something.

Now I understand why Lance does what he does.

"I need to get a hold of Lance right now. I better go over to his site and talk to him. Marge, please cancel my afternoon appointments. I have a very important matter to attend to."

"Yes, Mrs. Metzler. Is there anything I can do for you?" asked Marge.

"Yes, pray." Linda replied.

"Pray?" *What is going on?* Marge said to herself.

Linda found Lance and motioned for him to come over to the car.

"What is it, Linda? I am very busy," Lance said abruptly.

"I don't know what's happening, but this morning I hit a little girl on the way to work. She is okay, but she and her mother are homeless and I have an overwhelming desire to help them and other homeless families. I spoke with Marty Glenn and he has a property on Second Avenue that is for sale that could be used for a homeless shelter. He said the sellers want to have me sign papers at 4:00 pm to purchase this building. I know this is crazy, but what do you think? I am sure you could help renovate it if needed." stated Linda.

"I am stunned!' Lance replied.

"I know. This is so unlike me, but now I understand why you do what you do. I want to be part of it. The building is a really good price and I know we could swing it. I will then give the building to the Rescue Mission that runs the other homeless shelter. I really want to do this." Linda said, so excited.

"How could I say no? Let's go for it. I am so proud of you, sweetheart. We will talk more at home. Love you." Lance said.

Linda got on the phone right away to let Marty know she would be there at 4:00 pm to sign the papers.

"That's great. See you then." Marty said.

CHAPTER 8

"You are now the proud owner of 1010 W. Second Avenue, Linda. What are you going to do with it? asked Marty curiously.

"I am giving this building to the Rescue Mission to open another homeless shelter." Linda replied.

"What suddenly made you decide to do this?" inquired Marty.

"Oh, you wouldn't believe the day I have had. Let's just say it was divinely inspired, okay?" quipped Linda.

"Whatever you say."

When Linda had finished signing all the papers, she went over to the Rescue Mission with the good news.

"You're what?" exclaimed Director Jane Summers. "You are giving us another building?"

"That's right" said Linda. "There are only two things I ask. First, that the shelter be named Shepherd's Haven, and second, that Candace and Marie Morgan, who are currently staying at the Victoria Motel, be the first occupants," explained Linda.

"I don't see that being a problem. May I ask why such a generous gesture?" asked Jane.

"For once in my life, I want to make a difference, not just money."

Linda actually beat Lance home and was making dinner when everyone else arrived.

"Mom, you're home early and making dinner. What's the occasion?" asked Matthew.

"I'll tell you at dinner. Right now, please get washed up and set the table."

"Sure, mom." said Matthew.

"Well, I have had quite a day. This morning, I hit a little girl while on my way to work. She is okay, but it turns out she and her mom are homeless and lived in a cardboard box in the nearby alley," said Linda.

"Oh, wow, mom. I can't believe people are living in cardboard boxes. Where are they now?" asked Matthew.

"After the little girl was checked out at the hospital," Linda explained, "I had a cab take them to the Victoria Motel for now. I was surprised to find out there is only one homeless shelter in town, so I called Marty and he found a building for sale that could be used for another homeless shelter. Believe it or not, I was able to buy it, and I turned the building over to the Rescue Mission this afternoon. I have never felt so good in all my life."

"This is so cool, mom," Maggie said.

"You are right, Maggie. I know I have been so focused on making money that I have neglected my family. Well, no more. You are the most precious things in my life and I don't want to take you all for granted again. I will be home for dinner, come to your school events, and we can be a real family," Linda said with tears in her eyes.

"You don't know how happy I am to hear you say this," Lance said.

"I was seriously thinking of filing for divorce, but no more. I think we will be stronger than ever. I love you so much." Lance smiled.

"Group hug," said Matthew.

"Absolutely," Linda said. That hug lasted for several minutes.

Two weeks later, Shepherd's Haven was officially opened with the help of Lance's company and lots of donations. Linda and family was there to welcome Candace and Marie.

"How can we ever repay you?" asked Candace.

"You can do two things for me. I want Marie to be enrolled at Joshua's elementary school and for you to go over to Sam's Cafe in my office building and apply for a waitress job he has open. I have already put in a good word for you. Okay?" asked Linda.

"Okay, and thank you." Candace was trying not to cry.

Marie came over to Linda and gave her a big hug.

"Thank you for my medicine and my new home," Marie said.

"You are very welcome. I expect to be invited to your school events and your graduation, you know," Linda said.

"No problem," Marie said joyfully.

After getting settled in, Candace sat on her new bed and suddenly remembered her prayer the day Marie was hit by Linda's car.

"Thank you, God, for answering my prayer so beautifully," whispered Candace.

"You are welcome."

Printed in the United States
By Bookmasters